What Once Was Mine

What Once Was Mine

What Once Was Mine

Christina Louise

Pen2Pad Ink Publishing

What Once Was Mine

Library of Congress Cataloging–In–Publication Data

Name: Worth, Christina, author.
Title: What Once Was Mine/
Christina Worth

ISBN: 978-1-970135-87-9 Paperback

Published in the United States by
Pen2Pad Ink Publishing.
www.pen2padink.org

Requests to publish work from this book or to contact the author should be sent to:

What Once Was Mine

Preface

Hey guys! It's me, Lalani Elizabeth Jones. It's been a while so I'm checking back in with you. I know most of us are familiar with the introduction of a story giving a brief glimpse of what to look forward to. Well, if you haven't figured it out by now, I like to do things my own way!

You are a product of your environment. You live, and you learn. All great sayings you have heard. I do believe that we are a product of our environment. That looks different for each of us as individuals. However, at what point do you stop being a product of your environment and become a product of your decisions? As we move through this thing called life, our encounters should enlighten us and influence our evolution as a person. What kind of product are you right now? Are you proud of the product?

My life is far from perfect. Honestly, I am working on forgiving myself for a lot of the decisions I made. I present my life to you-humbly, openly, and truthfully. Yes, you are about to experience the greatest rollercoaster of emotions, but I promise the ride will be worth it.

Enjoy,

Lalani

Chapter 1

Time has really flown by. It's been about 18 months since I spoke with Donovan. Once my eyes were open, I never saw him the same again. I appreciate the journey now. It was painful, but I am a better person because of it. Donovan will make a great guy for someone. That someone however is not me.

So what new adventures am I experiencing? This chapter of my life starts with self-care and classes for my Master's degree. I'm only taking one class so I can pace myself. It doesn't matter how long it takes for you to finish. The goal is to finish. My twins are doing great, and I'm on a health kick. My eating habits have changed, and I work out daily. Hey...it takes work to keep this body fine like aged wine.

However, it would be 'too much like right' for me not to have some colorful moments along the way. It started with a walk along the beach of Pensacola Bay on a Thursday evening. The sun is setting on the gorgeous day. I have a Bushwhacker (Crushed ice, Vanilla ice cream, Kahlua Chocolate Liqueur with a shot of 151) in one hand and a pretzel in the other. (Uh...don't judge me...this was my 'me' time.) Sounds like a romantic scene from a movie, huh? Too bad it was a mini nightmare!

My beautiful walk was interrupted by this bold seagull. He tried to take my pretzel! I started running! Then, this bold seagull called his little gangsta friends to help. Now I'm running from a gang of seagulls while trying to hold onto my pretzel! (Look...I paid for that pretzel, and I planned to eat my pretzel. Plus, it was like a scene from the movie *Birds*! Ok... maybe I am over exaggerating, but still... there were a lot of seagulls!) I wasn't winning this battle with the birds until a deep smooth voice started shooing the birds away. Now where has this person been all this time? I know somebody saw me running along this beach with a flock of birds after me. That would kind of be hard to miss. I turned around to make a snide remark, but no words came out. I turned to see him: a 6'5, translucent, clean cut, arm tattoos, athletic build, beautiful eyes, and lips of a Greek god. He obviously drank enough water for both of us. His smile could remove any ounce of frustration I would ever have.

"Are you ok?" He asked. In my mind, I replied, but the signal never made it to my lips.

"Are you ok?" He asked again.

"Yes! Yes! I... I'm sorry. I'm ok," I said snapping back to reality. "The seagulls were determined to make me share my pretzel with them, and they won."

"Just checking. I'm Thomas."

"Lalani. Nice to meet you. Thank you again for helping me. I appreciate it." I said unlocking my car door.

"No problem."

"Is there something else?" I asked.

"No. Just wanted to make sure you

made it to your car safely." He answered. He opened my car door and closed it after I was safely in the car.

"Thank you...again." I answered.

"Pleasure to meet you, Lalani. Be careful out here with pretzels, ok?"

"I can work on that." I answered. I watched him jog away before I backed out of my parking spot. Maybe those seagulls weren't so bad after all.

Chapter 2

I thought I lost my moment to get to know Thomas better. I guess Fate was like "Wait for it...I got you!" Two weeks later, I drove a couple of hours to Blanche Outlet Mall. I figured retail therapy was safer than a Bushwhacker and a pretzel. I was walking out of Cherry's Boutique when I saw that 6'5 body again. It was Thomas with another gentleman. Thomas' friend was around 6'3, dark chocolate with the body of an NFL running back. The sight of these two reminds you that the body is an absolute temple, and I'm grateful when black men take the time to take care of it!

"Hey Stranger." I said as I tapped Thomas on the shoulder. He turned around. Once our eyes met, the biggest grin came across his face. "Thomas, right?" I asked.

"Yeah...I mean Yes! Good to see you again, Miss Lalani." He answered.

"You remembered by name?" I asked, surprised.

"Of course. I wanted to get your number that day. I wished I got your number that day." He said. His eyes were surveying my entire body until his friend intentionally coughed really loud. "Forgive me, Lalani. This is my brother, Raymond."

"So... you are the beautiful lady my brother has been raving about for the past two weeks?" Raymond asked. Thomas gave him a good nudge.

I laughed. "Did Thomas tell you how we met?"

"Yeah. I'm glad he stepped in with the gang of angry seagulls. He said that you wanted that pretzel!" Raymond stated while laughing. (It was a hilarious moment now, but then I was embarrassed.)

"Well I just wanted to say hello, Thomas. You guys enjoy the rest of your day." I said and turned to leave.

"Wait! How about you and Thomas talk some more. I'll catch up with you later Bro." Raymond said while slowly walking away.

"Nice to meet you Raymond!" I said.

"Same. I'm sure I'll be seeing more of you." Raymond said while literally almost sprinting away. Thomas and I found an empty bench under a tree where we sat and talked for hours. It was like we knew each other for years. We talked until the last store at the outlet closed. We finally decided to get up and leave. Thomas walked me to my car.

"Well... I have to get home. Let's exchange numbers. Maybe we can do this again." I said.

"We will. I promise that. Plus, I should hear from you soon. Can you let me know when you get home safely?" Thomas asked, smiling.

"Of course." I answered smiling. We exchanged numbers, and I started my car. When he was out of sight, I called my sister, Nicole, and told her what happened all the way until I got home. Once I made it home, I settled in for the night and gave Thomas a call. We literally talked until sunrise the next morning. Thankfully, it was the weekend, so I could sleep in. I learned that Thomas was in his late 30s, had no children, was never married, and was the oldest of 4 children. He was a retired Army vet that currently works as a firefighter.

We started talking and texting every day. I learned he didn't live that far from me and Raymond was his roommate. Even though Thomas knew where I lived, I went to his place. Since we were still getting to know each other, I was not in a rush to introduce him to my children. He understood that because he was just as protective of his nieces and nephews. Every time I came to visit Raymond would have the most amazing meals prepared. "He's trying to make sure I keep you smiling, your belly full, and your heart happy. He's already advised me that you are his new best friend." Thomas said with a smirk on his face while shaking his head.

After about a month and a half, Thomas and I decided to make it official and exclusive. I honestly wasn't entertaining anyone else anyway. However, healthy communication is key to making sure we were both on the same page. When it was time for him to meet the twins, he was so nervous. I gave him a pep talk to try to calm his nerves. The three of them instantly hit it off. He was such a big kid himself, so he fit right in with them. Once the evening was over, the kids went on and on about how much fun they had. From that moment on, the kids pretty much went with us wherever we went. Thomas would always ask for the kids when he would have his nieces and nephews over for the weekend. On those weekends, I would make the most of my time alone (movies, spa days, messages, retail therapy, etc.)

Raymond would join me sometimes if he wasn't busy for my weekends of self-care. This was the perfect time for me to learn even more about Thomas and Raymond. Raymond was metro-sexual. He paid attention to every intricate detail of his appearance from head to toe. He was extremely organized and structured. He did have some feminine characteristics, but he grew up in a house filled with women: His mother was a single parent, and he was her youngest out of three children.

Raymond was a complete gentleman. No matter where we went, women flocked to him. He was a habitual dater. None of his relationships lasted a long time.

"Why don't your relationships last long? Do none of these ladies pique your interest enough for you to want more with them?" I asked one day while we were having lunch.

"I know what I'm looking for. I... I just haven't found it yet. They are all beautiful women. I just haven't found the right one yet." He answered.

Raymond became my new best friend. I was always busy with the kids, school, and work. Making friends in Florida was difficult until I met him.

Chapter 3

It has been 8 blissful months for Thomas and me. Our families gel so well together. We talked about marriage, kids, and the future. We use words like "we" and "us". We've met each other's families, and we just seem to fit together perfectly. I know it sounds simple, but consistency in communication is something I love in a relationship. Well, consistency is something something both of us long for based on our past.

Thomas met his dad completely by accident. His father told him that his mom never informed him she was pregnant. By the time he found out, she was married and carrying a huge grudge. So, she purposely kept Thomas away from his dad. When Thomas confronted his mother about what his dad said, she reluctantly admitted that Thomas' father was telling the truth.

All of Thomas' siblings had different fathers. His mom's first marriage was to a man to help him get a green card. During the marriage, his mom had Ashley, his baby sister. The marriage was abusive, and Thomas often felt neglected. After the green card was official, the marriage was over, and Thomas had to become the man of the house at a very young age. When we would share moments of our past, he always said that he wanted better for our relationship and children. I could definitely relate.

Thomas was working toward a promotion in his rank with the fire department. When he received the promotion, he found out he would have to complete training at a remote location prior to beginning his new role. I decided to plan a celebration for him before he left since his birthday was three weeks away. Raymond helped me plan the surprise 'All-White' Boat party by reaching out to Thomas' family and close friends. I also invited my family too, and Nicole came to town early to help me. It was stressful, but definitely worth it.

"Surprise!" Everyone yelled once we

made it to the main deck of the yacht. Thomas was speechless. He even shed a tear.

"This...is for me?" He asked me.

"Yes, Lovebug. All for you. I really do appreciate you. You deserve it. Enjoy." I replied with a kiss. Thomas went around hugging family members and friends. The Cha-Cha Slide played and everyone lost their mind. It was a beautiful night with a beautiful person. The stress was definitely worth it.

Nicole and I went downstairs and grabbed the gifts so Thomas could open them. When we got back to the deck, everybody was mysteriously quiet. I looked around to see what everyone was looking at. The crowd parted for me to see Thomas and twins all on one knee. I dropped the gifts. Behind him were people holding balloons that spelled out WILL YOU MARRY ME? I looked at the twins. They had the proudest expressions on their faces.

"Lalani, you are love. Every moment with you has been something out of a dream. Your love for yourself, your kids, your village, and for me has been a true blessing to my life. Will you marry me?"

"Yes." I said quietly. The crowd erupted into shouts of joy and happiness. Thomas placed a 5-carat princess cut diamond with a rose gold band on my left ring finger. I bent down, grabbed his face, and gave him the softest kiss of gratitude.

"Thank you." I whispered. He smiled and stood up. Josiah and Lola grabbed my sides and we stood there for a minute in our own little bubble of contentment. The world disappeared. All I heard was four heartbeats in sync beating.

"Hold on. I'm not finished," Thomas started, "Lola. Josiah. I know I'm not your dad, and I will never want to replace him in your life. But...I want the chance to be a part of yours. Will you allow me to marry your mom?" He asked while pulling out a box with two gold bands with the word "Family" engraved on each band.

Lola's eyes widened to the size of saucers. "Yes!" She shouted happily and hugged Thomas.

"Hmmm…. I don't know," Josiah said jokingly. "Is that real gold?" Everyone laughed.

"Yes, it's real gold, dude. I checked." Thomas answered.

"Alright… I guess it's cool." Josiah said. Thomas and Josiah did their special handshake and they hugged. My smile was to the moon. I don't remember when that party ended. I do remember dancing in Thomas' arms and hoping that moment would never end.

But we had to return to reality. The time had come for Thomas to leave for three weeks. We were like two lovesick puppies on the day of his departure. I know they say that distance makes the heart grow fonder, but damn that! I wanted my well-earned fiancé here. Fortunately, Facetime would make it easier for us to see each other.

A week and a half had passed. We were almost there. Thomas would text whenever he had a moment. Once my workday ended, school work was completed, and kids were asleep, we would talk until I fell asleep. As he got closer to the end of the three weeks, I didn't hear from him as much. I assumed that the training was taking more of his time, so I just texted him to see how his day was going.

Thomas' response: Who is this?

My Response: Lalani, your fiancée

Thomas' response: Nothing

I called Raymond. He said he did not talk to him as well. A chill went down my spine as I explained what happened to Raymond.

"Hmmm... something about this does not make sense." Raymond said.

"That's it. I'm going to Louisiana." I replied.

"Now hold on there, partner. Before we waste gas, let's call the hotel first. Then, local hospitals and the police department. You don't need to be on anybody's road in your feelings."

"Ok. We will do this your way first." I answered. I called the hotel on 3-way with Raymond, and the guest service clerk transferred me to his room.

"Hello?" A woman answered. I hung up the phone.

"I know damn well they transferred me to the wrong room." I replied.

"Lani? Breathe. Just call again." Raymond suggested. I called back.

"Hello?" The same woman answered.

"Hello? Is...this Thomas James' room?" I asked, confused.

"Yes. He stepped out for a minute. Would you like to leave a message for him?" The woman asked.

"Tell him to call his fiancée, Lalani when he returns. I expect to hear from him before sunrise." I hung up the phone without even giving her a chance to respond.

Chapter 4

"Hey babe. It's not what you think." Thomas said. He called 10 minutes after I hung up on whoever that was.

"Ok. Explain please." I said.

"My phone was ruined. I couldn't call. The car broke down. Training has been intense. Bianca is just a friend." Thomas rambled. I heard him, but all the words seem to just run together. No one is perfect, and Thomas was not an exception. But... I... I felt like he was the perfect man for me. He wasn't the best at setting and keeping a budget. Plus, his social drinking habits were the worst. Nonetheless, those were two struggles I didn't mind. I know that every relationship has its trials, but this was a situation I could not process. Things didn't make sense.

"Can we talk about this when I get home? Please? I ordered a replacement phone that should be arriving any day now. Just allow me a chance to explain..." He continued rambling.

"Ok." I answered and hung up the phone.

Raymond was attached to my hip for the next couple of days. He never left me. Nicole called me several times a day. I told them I was ok, but I was honestly struggling. Thomas called every chance he got since his replacement phone came in, but our conversations were strained. I didn't know what to say. The space I once felt safe in was not uncertain and unstable.

When Thomas did return home, Raymond took the twins for the weekend. Thomas' first night back was awkward and cold. I turned my back to him when we were in bed and stared at the wall. Thomas moved closer to me, and I tensed up.

"Babe...I...I need to tell you something, and I don't know how you will take it." Thomas said.

"Ok. Talk." I said still facing the wall.

"The transmission went out on my car, and I ended up stranded on the side of the road while it was pouring down raining. My phone was in my pocket while I was in the rain, and I got completely soaked. Bianca was driving by. She was the only person kind enough to stop and give me a ride to the nearest bar to call for help. She stayed with me until my car was towed, and then she dropped me off at the hotel. That's all that happened."

I turned over and looked at him blankly.

"Say something...please." He pleaded.

"I don't know what to say. What are you expecting from me? We just got engaged and not even a month later we are dealing with this. I don't have anything to explain. You do. So, continue. Explain." I stated.

"You are right. I do need to explain. During the ride to my hotel, I told Bianca about our engagement. Then, she shared with me that she was fired from her job. Since she is here on a work visa, she will be forced to return to Ghana. I told her that

I felt bad for her, and I wished I could do something for her. As I was getting out of her car, she stopped me and asked if I would marry her so she would not have to leave."

"And what the hell did that have to do with you?" I asked, sitting up in bed.

"Well, she offered me a large payout if I would marry her so she could get her green card. I told her that I couldn't do that, and I got out of her car. Then, she... she started showing up to the hotel... every day... trying to get me to reconsider. I finally told her I would help her find another way. When you called the room, I left to get a soda from the vending machine, and she answered the phone. That was it. That was the only time she was in the room." I let Thomas' words sink in before I answered. He didn't have to tell me what happened. Plus, to come up with a story like this is a lot. Like... a lot a lot.

"I believe you. Thank you for telling me. You haven't done anything in the past to make it seem like I shouldn't believe you. But...you know how important communication is to me. No matter how painful... you have to talk to me, okay?" I asked.

"Yeah...I understand. Thank you."

"Now is there anything else you want to tell me?" I asked.

"Well...yeah. So, you know Raymond and I have been friends for a long time.... since we were kids." Thomas started.

"Yeah. It's good to have friendships like that."

"True. But... there's more to our friendship."

"What do you mean 'more'?"

"Well," Thomas said, taking a deep breath, "Raymond has been there for me in every way possible...even...physically."

I paused and tried to think of what Thomas was trying to say. "You mean... like working out?"

"Nah... more intimately." Thomas said quietly. Oxygen stopped traveling out of my mouth. I started coughing heavily and gasping for air at the same time. "I need air." I managed to get out before getting out of bed and opening the patio window sliding door. The cold night air slapped my face back to reality. Once my breathing went back to normal, I came back into the room where Thomas gave me a bottle of water. I sat on the bed and tried to muster up words.

"So... you mean that you and Raymond had sex?" I asked.

"Yes. Twice: once when I was a teenager and again when I moved in with him several years ago. Both times I was in a dark place in life. Raymond pretty much knows everything about me. He never judges me." Thomas explained.

"So... are you gay?"

"No, I'm not gay or bisexual. It was just what I needed at that moment. That's all." Thomas said staring up at me from the floor. He reached for my hand, but I pulled away.

"I need you to get your things and

leave." I stated.

"But Lani--"

"Thomas. Leave. Now." He got up and put on clothes. He grabbed a duffel bag from the closet and started packing quietly. I sat on the side of bed in pure disbelief. Did he...was I... how did...

"Lani, I know this is a lot. I just thought you should know everything. No secrets. Communication. Since we getting married--"

"Thomas. Stop. Just stop. I need a minute and your talking is making it hard for me to find that minute in the midst of the haze that is fogging my thoughts. Leave. Please."

He picked up his duffle bag. "Ok. But I will be back. I love you, and I'm not giving up on us." Thomas said before closing the door behind him.

Chapter 5

"Raymond. Bring my kids home, please."
I asked.

"Uh...ok. Here we come. See you in a bit." Raymond said and hung up the phone. I went to the mirror and tried to put myself together before my kids came back. I swear I feel like I'm in the Twilight Zone. Thomas was supposed to be different. He was supposed to be better. My thoughts were interrupted by the doorbell ringing.

"Hi Mom." Lola said sleepily.

"Why did we have to leave Uncle Raymond's? We were sleep." Josiah asked, rubbing his eyes.

I kissed them both on the forehead. "I'm sorry babies. Go to sleep. I'll check on you all later." Lola and Josiah headed to their room. Raymond came back from the kitchen by the time the kids were in their room.

"You ok?" Raymond asked.

"Ask your brother...or should I say your boyfriend." I snapped.

"Wait...what?" Raymond asked.

"Ask Thomas. He will tell you everything you need to know like always. Now you leave. Good night."

"Uh...ok? Good night." Raymond said. I locked the door after he left, checked on the twins, and used the rest of my energy to collapse onto my bed. I remained in bed the rest of the weekend. Thankfully, there were leftovers in the fridge, and the kids are big enough to use a microwave. I gathered enough strength to go to work that Monday morning, but each day of the week was a struggle. As a single mom, I didn't have the luxury of being able to take time to process my emotions. I had a ton of missed calls, voice messages, and texts from Thomas, Raymond, and Nicole.

A week passed, and I started to regain my balance. I told Nicole I would call her soon. Raymond let me know that he and Thomas talked. Raymond wanted a chance to explain himself. Thomas did the most: texting, calling, sending flowers, and more. I wasn't ready to deal with him yet.

The weekend came, and I survived, thank God! I invited Raymond over to the house so we could talk.

"Wine?" I said, opening the door with a glass.

He smiled and took the glass. "Thank you for hearing me out."

"Thank you for your patience. I just needed time to get my head together."

"Yeah...I can understand that. You feeling better?"

"Eh.... I'm here. That's all I can give you right now."

"Understandable. Listen...I... I didn't want to tell you. I felt like that was something for Thomas to tell you in his own time. I didn't want to get involved in your relationship, but I apologize for any

chaos it caused. Thomas is NOT gay. But...
I am."

I looked up from my glass. "Are you serious?"

"Yeah. I've known for years. Just didn't know how to tell everyone. I questioned what would happen if I did: Will they accept me? What happens if they don't? I know I can date any woman I want...but that's not my truth. I date them because that's the image everyone has for me. Thomas is the only one who knows."

"Wow. Just...wow."

"Yeah."

"Raymond, there is power and freedom in your truth. You are an intriguing human being! Your sexual preference doesn't change how amazing you are. I love you just for being you."

"Really?"

"No... for fake. Of course, I do! I will always encourage you to walk in your truth when you are ready, and I will support you along the way. When you are ready, I will be there as your biggest cheerleader!"

"Lani...thank you. Just...thank you." He gave me that drop-dead smile with tears coming down his eyes.

"I love you too honey! Own your truth. You will be surprised how it will help others." I gave him the biggest hug.

"Well...speaking of truths...what about Thomas?"

I took a large sip of my wine with huge eyes. "What about him?"

"Thomas loves you...dearly. He wouldn't do anything to lose what you two got. Give him another chance... please?"

"Let us get through this movie, and I'll think about it." I answered. I wanted to enjoy this moment with a friend. My relationship issues could wait two hours.

Raymond left after the movie, and I decided to deal with Thomas. I called him, and he must have been staring at the phone because he picked up on the first ring.

"Hey babe. You ok? The kids good? Do you need anything? How was your day?"

"Thomas...breathe," I chuckled, "I'm ok. The kids are fine. We don't need anything, and my day was fine. I, uh, was calling to see if you could come over so we could talk."

"Yes! Of course! I will be there. Oooo...Thank you God for answering my prayers! Glory! Do you need me to pick up anything before I get there?"

"No. Just yourself. I'll see you tomorrow." I hung up and laughed. He probably went into a complete shouting session like Mr. Brown from The Madea movies. I turned the TV off and went to bed. For the first time in about a week, I actually slept the entire night. I slept so peacefully that I woke up to two big lumps in my bed: Lola and Josiah. I kissed my little lumps on the head. I made a lot of mistakes in this life, but these two were not one of them. They were my greatest accomplishments.

It was a super comfy Saturday, so I made breakfast. Then, we lounged around the house and watched movies. A knock around noon interrupted our comfy Saturday.

"Who is it?" Josiah asked.

"Thomas!"

Josiah threw the door open and ran into Thomas' arms. "Dude! Where have you been?"

"What it is, Josiah? I've been working!"

"We missed you." Lola said, hugging Thomas.

"I missed you too!" Thomas responded.

"Guys...go to your room so Thomas and I can talk." I walked them to their rooms and closed their doors. I walked back into the living room to a nervous Thomas rubbing his hands together."
"Hey," I started, "Thank you for coming."

"Thank you for calling. I know you

needed time to digest everything."

"Yeah...it was a lot. I spoke with Raymond. He confirmed that nothing is going on between the two of you. However, you two did have those two moments in your past. I'm not your judge or jury, but I can't help but question everything about our relationship."

He nodded his head. "I can understand that. But I am willing to do anything to make things work between us. My life is so much better when you and the kids are in it. I told you about my past because I didn't want any secrets. To lose you would mean losing my lifeline. I...I can't apologize enough for the poor decisions with Bianca. I will never stop trying to regain your trust, baby. Never."

"I appreciate that. But...I still feel like we need counseling. You are carrying a lot of pain from your past, and this present incident has made an impact on our relationship. I want us to be healthy physically, mentally, and emotionally."

"Sure, babe. Whatever it takes. I want to be the best that I can be for you, the kids, and myself. The next couple of weeks will be hectic as I transition into my new role, but I'll make it work.

Chapter 6

It's been about two months, and we have grown stronger as a unit. Thomas' work days were longer, but the communication between us was indescribable. He made time to call and text throughout the day just to make sure we were good. He really was my best friend. I finally feel like everything makes sense, and I am receiving the happiness and peace I deserve. I also had time to enroll in classes again so I can continue with my Master's Degree along with my new job. It also seems like I wasn't the only person who wanted to embark on a new type of life.

"So... I need your help. I've decided to come out to my family, and I want you to be there." Raymond explained.

"Wow. Really?" I asked.

"Yes. I've thought about it. I want the

freedom to just be me. It takes so much energy to keep this image up. Honestly, I'm tired. I go to bed alone at night because I'm afraid of what people will think of me. I know what the Bible says. I prayed many times for God to take these feelings away, but I still have them. Am I bad?"

"Are you bad? Of course not! God never said we would be exempt from experiencing bad things. When Paul had the thorn in his side, he begged God to remove it. God said that His grace was sufficient, and that same grace is extended to you. You are not a mistake. God can only create extraordinary people including you. This world needs you in your truest form and the purpose that lies within you. I will gladly go with you to share this with your family. Just let me know when and where."

"What would I do without you, Lani?"

"Have bad taste in wine." We laughed and hugged each other. I traveled with Raymond the following week to be his support system. Most of his family was not surprised at the news. When he came back to the city and told friends, some stayed while others left. No matter the reaction, I was his biggest supporter. I was overjoyed. So many people live their lives in secret due to the fear of being alone and rejected. Raymond no longer had to hide behind his truth.

Thomas and I decided on a fall wedding. Raymond and Nicole have been in overdrive assisting me with everything. Days turned into weeks, and weeks turned into months. Before I knew it, the wedding was three months away. Thomas and I started marriage counseling. Most of the planning was completed. Things were shaping up to be on track for us to move into a new part of our lives. Thomas and I were intentional about our growth as a couple. We equipped ourselves with healthy tools for our marriage as well as ourselves individually.

Two months before the wedding, however, I started to feel... well... weird. Thomas' behavior began to change, and I was not the only victim. Raymond and everyone else noticed it too. I tried to have a normal conversation with Thomas, but he gave me one-word responses. I sent an edible arrangement to his fire station, but the delivery guy said he was not there. I called Thomas' phone, and it went straight to voicemail. When I asked him about work, he lied to me! I took a walk so that I could call Raymond.

"Hey honey. Has Thomas said anything to you about something going on with him?" I asked.

"No. But...he has been acting funny. Very secretive. Doesn't really want to talk anymore. If he comes to the house, he's in and out. If I ask him to hang out, he has an excuse why he can't." Raymond explained.

"Wait...how long has it been since you two hung out? He told me you two were kicking it."

"Must be another Raymond. We haven't hung out in almost two months now. I just chalked it up to his job and his new position."

"Hmmm. Ok. Thanks love."

"Uh...Lani...you good friend?"

"Yeah. I'll talk to you later." I hung up the phone and went into detective mode. He's lying about work, lying about Raymond, and he's away from me. Before I jumped to conclusions, I decided to give him the benefit of the doubt. I found him in bed when I got home from my walk.

"Hey Lovebug. Everything ok?" I asked.

"No babe. I'm ok. Everything with the wedding has me on edge. I just want everything to be perfect for you." He answered. The hell? This bastard lied again even without blinking! I've been handling the wedding planning with Raymond and Nicole. Something wasn't right, and I wasn't going to stop until I knew what happened.

Chapter 7

"Never let your left hand know what your right hand is doing." My grandmother always said that. I didn't understand it then, but I do now.

I took some days off to do research just to make sure I wasn't completely crazy. I didn't tell anyone. Lola and Josiah led normal lives like nothing was wrong. I let Thomas leave like normal for work, but I left shortly after him. I followed him, and he stopped at a house 20 minutes away from our apartment. Thomas gets out of the car with his bag, a woman opens the door to the house, and she greets him with a hug and kiss. I took a picture of the woman and called in a favor from an old school classmate, Claire, who is now a private investigator to find out more about this mystery woman he was obviously cheating with.

For the next couple of days, I acted like

everything was normal. Thomas and the kids left every day. Thomas called like he normally would, and I continue to pretend like I was oblivious to his other life. Claire finally called to tell me what she found out.

"I hope you are sitting down for this." Claire started.

"Well...the acting I've been doing for the past three days could rival Halle Berry. Sitting down should not be as hard. What did you find out?"

"So, the lady in the picture is named Bianca Smith. They have known each other for a while since he went to training in Louisiana?"

So that's the same woman, I thought to myself. "Really? What else did you find out?"

"Well...that she's kind of his wife...for the past two months."

"Married?" I mustered to get out.

"Yep. I emailed you a copy of the

marriage certificate. It's probably because of the baby."

"The Baby!" I shouted.

"Yeah. I sent you a sonogram in the same email. I'm sorry, Lani." Claire said.

I sat quietly trying to process everything. Married? A baby? How the hell did he...How could he? "I... I gotta go, Claire. Thank you." I hung up the phone and sat in disbelief. He has an entire separate life with this woman. How in the hell is this possible?! We have been going to counseling and everything. Our wedding day is less than two months away, and he's already married. What the hell is this?! Why is this? Why me?! I have loved him for who he is, flaws and all. I have stood by him no matter what and this is what he thinks of me. My alarm on my phone took me out of my confusion and disbelief. It was almost time for the twins to come home. I texted Raymond and asked him to pick up the kids from school and take them to his house. I immediately received a phone call from him.

"Sis...what's going on?" Raymond

asked.

"He...He's married." I said in between tears.

"Who? Thomas?!"

"Ye...Yeah..."

"But...how...that's why he ain't talking to me!"

"Just...get the twins...please...I can't..."

"I got you." Raymond said and hung up. I opened the email notification on my phone to see it: the marriage certificate and the sonogram. My confusion turned into rage. I got up, went to our bedroom, and started tearing clothes down from the closet. I grabbed every box I could find, filled it with his stuff, and started placing it outside of the house. Then, I sent Thomas a text message with a screenshot of the marriage certificate and sonogram:

Congrats. Come get your stuff.

Thomas called immediately. "Lani... what are you talking about?"

"I know you are married. I know who Bianca is. I know you have a kid on the way. What I don't know is how long your stuff can last outside my house before it ends up in the dumpster."

"Lani...Please...Just me explain."

"Ok, Thomas, please enlighten me. Enlighten me on how in about two months you would have two wives!"

"About two months ago, Bianca reached out to me. She...She was still trying to figure out how to stay in the states. I told her we would meet over drinks to brainstorm. I guess we had too many drinks because I woke up the next morning at her place. She said that we had sex without protection. I tried to steer clear of her, but she called a couple of weeks later to tell me she was pregnant."

"So... you still went to see her KNOWING the hell we went through the last time?" I asked.

"I know... I know...I just...I didn't want to leave her like that. Plus, she needed her green card so she could raise our child here. I didn't love her. I don't love her. I just didn't want to lose you. It spiraled out of control so fast. I honestly didn't know what to do."

"Well was it worth it? I gave you my all: the good and the bad. I thought that we both had made an unwavering decision that we had each other's back no matter what and that we would love and protect each other. I honestly don't know what else to say to you so I'm not going to fake it. Keep the keys. I'm changing the locks. Despite all of this, I really do wish you the best. Take care Thomas." I hung up before he could respond.

Chapter 8

I had Toni Braxton's *Secrets* album on repeat. Every time "Unbreak My Heart" came on, I lost what little strength I had left. I get it. I understand why Toni had such pain in her voice. It hurts when you give someone so much of you, and they see no reason to take that into consideration when attempting to build a relationship with you. It just...hurts.

I ignored everyone's calls. Eventually, Raymond showed up at my house and refused to leave. I wanted to argue, but I had no energy to do so. I poured my energy into marriage counseling, so I stopped going to my personal counseling a long time ago. Raymond's presence helped. He held me every time I cried. He never tried to justify anyone's actions or choices. He was just...present. I needed that since I couldn't get out of the bed, and my appetite was non-existent. He also helped with Lola and Josiah so they wouldn't see their mom as screwed up as I really was.

A knock came to the door. "I'll get it." Raymond said. I stayed under the covers staring at the closet door. When he came back, Nicole was with him.

"What are you doing here?" I asked.

"Raymond called," She said, jumping in the bed to hug me. "I hope you didn't think you would go through this alone. I love you Sissy. You are one of the strongest people I know. It's ok to let others be strong for you. Let us do that now." Her words triggered another crying moment.

I extended my time off from work. Nicole got my counselor to make house calls which helped, but I still struggled. Didn't eat. Didn't drink. Sleeping was brief because nightmares kept me awake. I know Nicole and Raymond mean well, but I can handle this. If I can just take this...this...

Chapter 9

"See...I told you she was just asleep." Is that my mom?

I slowly opened my eyes, and my mom was here. With me. In a hospital room. I looked down to see tubes and IVs poking out of my skin. The last thing I remembered was standing in my shower. How did I end up here? And what is in my mouth?

"Excuse me. Can someone come to remove the feeding tube from my daughter's mouth?" My mom asked.

"Lola. Josiah. Let's go get something from the gift shop for your mom." I heard Raymond say. I couldn't move my head a lot, but I know that baritone voice anywhere. All I could see was Nicole on my left and my mom on my right.

"Well lookie who is awake! Good to see your eyes, Ms. Jones. Give us a couple of minutes and we will have that tube out of your mouth." The nurse said. I grabbed Nicole and my mom's hand as they slowly removed the tube. I heaved a little, but my breathing started to return to normal.

"What...what happened?" I asked hoarsely.

"You passed out from dehydration. We told you to eat, Lani." Nicole said.

"How long have I been out?"

"About a week." Mom answered.

"I... I..."

"I nothing. Relax, Lani. You are ok. I'm going to go and check on Raymond and the kids." Nicole said and left the room.

"Mom...I'm...I'm so sorry."

"Baby...what are you apologizing for?"

"I just..."

"Lalani...no matter what you have experienced I have always been proud of who you are. I love your compassion and strength. God knew you had more to do which is why you are still here with us. You have nothing to say sorry about. You needed rest. You finally got it. Now enjoy it." She explained patting my hand. I smiled faintly but happily. I am certain I have the power and support to move on.

Chapter 10

It's amazing how we don't break when we think we will. We are stronger than we believe, and a great village helps too. My mom stayed with me after I got out of the hospital. I needed to regain my energy and balance plus it gave her time with Lola and Josiah. I started my counseling sessions again. My heart was still hurting, but it wasn't bleeding out like it was before.

Far too often, we allow the brokenness we carry to consume the blessing that we receive in life. Thomas carried so much brokenness, and I took it on as my own when that was not my job. He still calls. I asked him once to respect my wishes by not calling and focusing on the life he created for himself. Fortunately, God saw fit to allow me a second chance, and I will NOT waste it. He also gave me an awesome friend, Raymond, who calls every day. And my sister, Nicole, who will probably move here soon based on how much she already visits. I am a strong believer that God never sends us into battle defenseless. We may not understand the weapon or tool at first, but we will as soon as the battle happens.

My life adventures are never a straight line from point A to point B. I have to take every side road and shortcut I think is good for me. It takes longer, but I'm grateful for the testimony it allows me to share with others. I consider my life.... uh...colorful. Yeah, that's it. Colorful. It is far from black and white, and I'm ok with that.

I'm still on the path to obtain my Master's Degree. Lola and Josiah are still amazing. I still love the idea of love. It's who I am. There is a 'happily ever after' for me out there. No trial is my end. It's more like a stepping stone towards my destiny. I am humbled to be alive to implement the lessons that I have learned. I'm still fine tuning this 'fine like aged wine' body back, but I am also taking the time to make sure that I am the best me that I can be. Don't be sad. I feel overjoyed to have the chance to work on my mind, body and soul. This is not a goodbye...just a see y'all later. Y'all are family now, especially since I'm putting all my business out there. Don't worry. I'm sure I will have something else to share with you. Until then, be amazing, be encouraged, but, most of all, be your best you!

Get Connected With Author Christina Louise On Social Media.

f Christina Louise

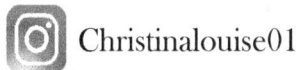 Christinalouise01

Other Books By This Author

Christina Louise